The sweetest drool-kiss is from Lisa Renee

N.R.

A thousand kisses for Carlijn

M.t.C.

Copyright © 2002 by Nanda Roep and Marijke ten Cate
Originally published by
Lemniscaat b.v. Rotterdam under the title *Kusje*
Printed and bound in Belgium
All rights reserved
CIP data is available
First U.S. edition

Kisses

Nanda Roep & Marijke ten Cate

Front Street ❦ Lemniscaat

Asheville, North Carolina

Lisa asks, "Will you give me a kiss?"
"Of course," Daddy says. "Do you want ...

... a witch's kiss?

... a butterfly kiss?

... a grandma kiss?

... a mom kiss?

... a vacation kiss?

... a monster kiss?

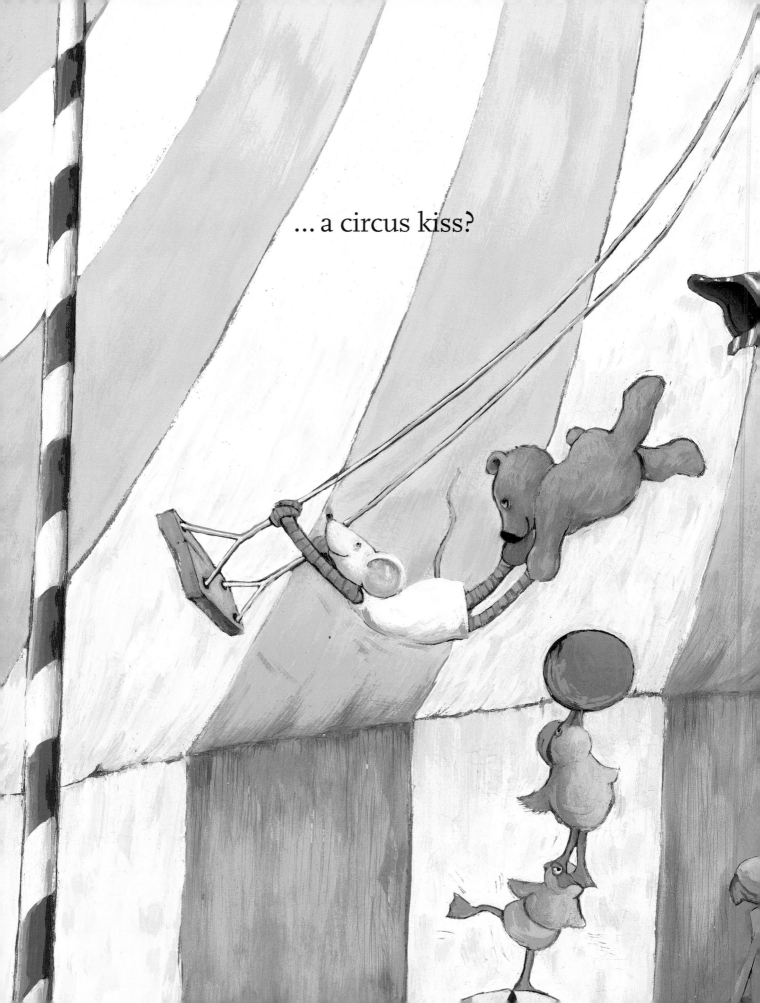

... a circus kiss?

... a birthday kiss?

... an Eskimo kiss?

Lisa laughs.

"No, Daddy, I want a *goodnight* kiss!"

"Oh, that kind of kiss!

"A kiss that makes your toes heavy.
A kiss that makes your fingers so limp they
can't even lift a feather.
A kiss that makes your eyes so tired
it's hard to keep them open," Daddy says.

... and Lisa falls asleep.